DOGS 101

By Rebecca Paley

Scholastic Inc.

New York   Toronto   London   Auckland
Sydney   Mexico City   New Delhi   Hong Kong

ISBN: 978-0-545-20731-7

12   11   10   9   8   7   6   5   4   3   2   10   11   12   13   14   15/0

Designed by Deena Fleming and Bill Henderson
Printed in the U.S.A.   40
First printing, August 2010

CONTENTS

IT'S A DOG'S WORLD . . .

. . . and thank goodness for that! There would be a lot less laughter, love, and wet, sloppy kisses without these funny, four-legged creatures to keep us company. No wonder they're considered man's best friend!

Today, there are 163 breeds recognized by the American Kennel Club®. And as anyone who watches *Dogs 101* knows, each one is unique. Some dogs are sporty and love to play fetch for hours. Others would rather spend the afternoon perched on their master's lap. There are cold-weather breeds, and breeds that love to soak in the sun. There are city dogs and country dogs, shy dogs and social dogs, high-maintenance dogs and dogs that barely need a thing.

In this book, you'll meet over twenty-five of the most popular breeds. There are many more, but this pick of the litter covers the major categories. If you have any doubt about which type of pooch is right for you, you'll finally be able to settle the question once and for all. There's even a quiz at the end to test your canine comprehension.

The more you know about these fascinating creatures, the more you'll enjoy them. Remember, it's a dog's world — we just live in it!

A WORD ABOUT DOG BREEDS

This book includes dogs that fall into seven main groups: sporting, hound, working, terrier, toy, nonsporting, and herding. Here's a quick overview of each.

Sporting

Sporting dogs were originally bred as hunters. Today, they are friendly, athletic family companions. Dogs in this group need lots of exercise and fresh air. The Cocker Spaniel, Irish Setter, and Labrador Retriever are all sporting dogs.

Hound

The hound group includes many different dogs with many different traits. Most are good hunting dogs with the good sense of smell needed to follow a trail. Some of these dogs also make an unusual sound called baying. This group includes the Basset Hound, the Beagle, the Bloodhound, and the Dachshund.

Working

Working dogs have been bred over the years to perform important jobs, such as guarding property, rescuing animals and people, and pulling sleds and carts. Working dogs tend to be smart and capable, and they make great companions. This group includes the Akita, the Doberman Pinscher, and the Saint Bernard.

Terrier

Terriers are all personality: they are energetic and exuberant. They were bred to hunt and kill rats and mice, so they don't have much tolerance for other animals. Terriers are fun pets, but their owners should be prepared for the occasional battle of wills. Some terriers are: the Airedale Terrier, Soft-Coated Wheaten Terrier, and the West Highland White Terrier.

Toy

Don't be fooled by the small size of these dogs — toys can be tough! But they're also quite charming, and their adorable looks win them many fans. Because of their size, toys are popular in big cities and with apartment dwellers. This group includes the Chihuahua, the Maltese, and the Poodle.

Nonsporting

This group includes many different dogs with many different personalities, sizes, coats, and appearances. The Chow Chow, Dalmatian, and French Bulldog are all nonsporting dogs.

Herding

Members of the herding group have one amazing ability: to control the movement of other animals. But as pets, most herding dogs never get to use this instinct — except on members of the family! These are smart dogs who are very easy to train and prove to be great companions. The Old English Sheepdog is a member of this group.

Name: AIREDALE
(AKA "KING OF THE TERRIERS")
Group: TERRIER

FAMILY FRIENDLINESS:
Airedales make excellent pets for an active family.

Size: Medium. About 2 feet tall; weighs up to 60 pounds

Coat: A nonshedding, double-layered coat

Coloring: A combination of black and tan

Origin: Airedales were first bred in northern England in the 1800s to hunt foxes, water rats, and other small game.

Temperament: Airedales are known for their extreme intelligence. Love and stimulation keep them happy and good-natured. Airedales don't always play nicely with other dogs.

Health: Apart from the occasional bone-joint issue, this hardy breed has very few health issues. Life span is ten to thirteen years.

★ Airedales have the largest teeth of all Terriers.

★ During World War I, Airedales served as messengers for the English army.

Famous owners:
PRESIDENTS WARREN G. HARDING, WOODROW WILSON, AND CALVIN COOLIDGE

Grooming: Airedales have long beards and pointy tails, so they must be brushed weekly. They also have to be hand-stripped two times a year. That means the dead, bristly undercoat of hair is plucked out by hand, which can take a while.

Environment: Airedales can adapt to most climates, but they need lots of exercise, so they do best in the country or in towns with plenty of park space.

Training: Some can be stubborn and headstrong, but if you start them as pups, they respond well to training.

Name: AKITA
Group: WORKING

Size: Big. More than 2 feet tall; weighs up to 130 pounds

Coat: A double coat: a coarse waterproof layer over a dense, woolly layer

Coloring: Just about any color, including white, brindle (brown with white streaks), and pinto (spotted)

Origin: Akitas began as hunters of bears, boar, and other big game in ancient Japan. They are known for their legendary sense of loyalty and tough, determined personalities.

Temperament: Akitas are considered high-risk pets — like the Pit Bull and the Rottweiler, they are known for biting and aggression. But with the right care, these strong, fierce dogs can be cuddly and lovable.

Health: Bred to climb steep mountains and trudge through deep snow, they're definitely hardy. But like all big dogs, they can suffer joint ailments and bloating, a life-threatening stomach problem. Their life span is ten to twelve years.

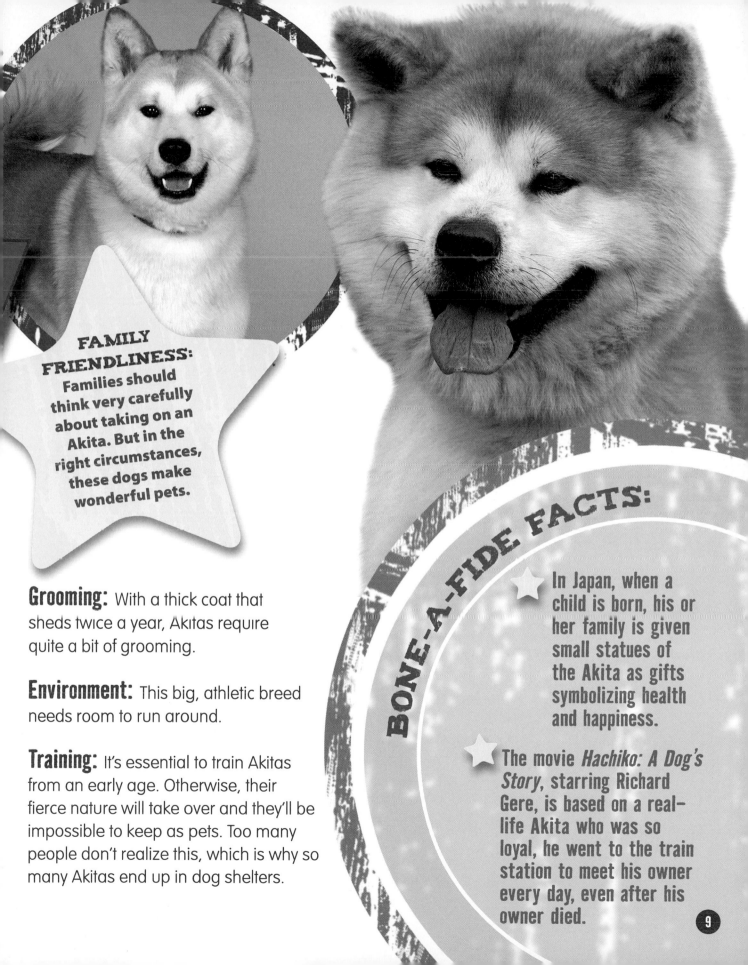

FAMILY FRIENDLINESS: Families should think very carefully about taking on an Akita. But in the right circumstances, these dogs make wonderful pets.

Grooming: With a thick coat that sheds twice a year, Akitas require quite a bit of grooming.

Environment: This big, athletic breed needs room to run around.

Training: It's essential to train Akitas from an early age. Otherwise, their fierce nature will take over and they'll be impossible to keep as pets. Too many people don't realize this, which is why so many Akitas end up in dog shelters.

BONE-A-FIDE FACTS:

★ In Japan, when a child is born, his or her family is given small statues of the Akita as gifts symbolizing health and happiness.

★ The movie *Hachiko: A Dog's Story*, starring Richard Gere, is based on a real-life Akita who was so loyal, he went to the train station to meet his owner every day, even after his owner died.

9

Name:

BASSET HOUND

Group: HOUND

Size: Small. About 14 inches tall; weighs between 40 and 60 pounds

Coat: Thick and tight

Coloring: Any combination of black, white, tan, or red

Origin: These dogs were bred by hunters in sixteenth-century France to track rabbits and other small game. The Basset Hound is built for tracking, with a powerful sense of smell and short legs that keep its nose and body close to the ground.

FAMILY FRIENDLINESS: Its gentle, loving nature makes the Basset Hound a perfect family pet. Basset Hounds love to go on walks, sniffing the ground as they go.

Temperament: Although they were bred to be hunting dogs, Basset Hounds have a very gentle disposition that makes them excellent companions.

Health: Life expectancy is around ten to thirteen years. Obesity is a problem, especially since it puts pressure on the long spine.

Grooming: Their short coat requires little grooming. But the Basset's wrinkly face needs to be cleaned regularly. Basset Hounds also have a tendency to drool.

Environment: These dogs adapt well to any climate.

Training: True to their hound nature, Bassets can be stubborn. But with early training, they learn to follow commands.

Famous owner: THE MARQUIS DE LAFAYETTE GAVE ONE TO PRESIDENT GEORGE WASHINGTON AFTER THE AMERICAN REVOLUTION.

BONE-A-FIDE FACTS!

⭐ The Basset Hound holds the record for the world's longest dog ears. Its sense of smell is second only to the Bloodhound's.

⭐ Those droopy ears are a big help during hunting. They drag along the scent that the dogs are tracking, keeping the dog stimulated.

Name: BEAGLE
Group: HOUND

Size: Small. About 15 inches tall; weighs no more than 30 pounds

Coat: Short-haired

Coloring: Any combination of black, brown, tan, white, and other colors

Origin: Beagles are an ancient breed, going all the way back to fifteenth-century England, where they were used to hunt rabbits and other small game.

Temperament: Beagles are friendly, gentle, and always up for an adventure. They are also extremely social, craving the company of people and other dogs.

Health: Beagles typically live for twelve to fifteen years, longer than most breeds. At some point, they often develop back problems.

Famous owner:
PRESIDENT LYNDON B. JOHNSON

Grooming: The Beagle's short coat doesn't need a lot of attention — Beagles don't shed much.

Environment: Although small, they like room to run around, preferring a house with a yard to a city apartment.

BONE-A-FIDE FACTS:

★ The Beagle's name probably comes from the French words for "open throat," because of the breed's loud, melodious howl.

★ One of the world's most lovable (and funniest) Beagles is Charlie Brown's dog, Snoopy.

Name: # BLOOD
Group: # HOUND

FAMILY FRIENDLINESS: Bloodhounds are not as playful as other hounds, but with the right family they make devoted pets.

Famous owner: ENGLAND'S QUEEN VICTORIA

HOUND

Temperament: While Bloodhounds are plenty affectionate, they can be shy and sensitive, especially around strangers. They don't always like to share with other dogs.

Health: Life expectancy is seven to ten years. This breed is particularly prone to bloating. Their ears and eyes can become infected if not cleaned regularly.

Grooming: Bloodhounds need a fair amount of grooming. Their coats must be brushed regularly, and their eyes, ears, and wrinkly faces must be kept clean. Plus, they drool a lot.

Environment: This breed adapts well to most climates. Despite their reputation for laziness, Bloodhounds like regular exercise.

Training: Bloodhounds tend to be stubborn, so it's important to establish the upper hand early. Be kind but firm with a Bloodhound, and he'll respond with love and obedience.

BONE-A-FIDE FACT:

Bloodhounds have the strongest sense of smell of any breed. That's why they are used by police to track criminals. They can smell a trail that's over 300 hours old. Evidence tracked by Bloodhounds has been accepted in court.

Size: About 2 feet tall; weighs 100 pounds or more. Bloodhounds are big dogs!

Coat: Loose. They are sometimes called "the dog in a baggy suit."

Coloring: Black and tan, liver and tan, and solid red

Origin: Bloodhounds, which have been around since at least the eighth century, have been popular in the United States since the early 1900s.

Name: CHIHUAHUA

Group: TOY

Size: Tiny. About 9 inches or under; no more than 6 pounds

Coat: Either short and smooth or long and glossy

Coloring: Tan, red, black, white, and splashed

Origin: This Mexican native has been around for centuries, making it one of the oldest breeds in the Americas.

FAMILY FRIENDLINESS: These loyal companions are recommended for families, but extra care must be taken to make sure small children are gentle with them.

Temperament: Extremely devoted to their owners. They are trainable, but only if you start early. Teaching a two- or three-year-old Chihuahua new tricks is next to impossible.

Health: If well cared for, a Chihuahua can easily live for fifteen to twenty years. But they are prone to overindulgence, leading to diabetes and bad knees, so watch their diet carefully. Chihuahuas also have a false sense of their own toughness, so you need to make sure they don't pick fights with larger dogs.

Grooming: Easy — nothing more than the occasional bath.

Environment: These dogs do not do well in cold climates. Their tiny size makes them great apartment pets.

Famous owners:
SOCIALITE PARIS HILTON, SINGER BRITNEY SPEARS, SINGER/ACTRESS HILARY DUFF

BONE-A-FIDE FACTS:

⭐ Chihuahuas are the smallest breed in the world.

⭐ Mexican royalty used Chihuahuas like hot-water bottles — to keep them warm in bed at night!

Name: CHOW

Group: NONSPORTING

Temperament: Because of its aloofness, this noble breed sometimes seems more like a cat than a dog. While they make loyal companions, they don't go out of their way to please, and can be standoffish toward strangers.

Health: Their life span is generally eight to twelve years. Keep an eye on their eyes — they're prone to an eye condition called entropion, which can lead to blindness if left untreated.

Grooming: Regular brushing and bathing is a must to keep the coat shiny, especially with rough-haired Chow Chows.

Environment: With their thick coats, Chow Chows don't do well in hot, humid conditions. They like a house with a yard where they can run regularly.

Training: Chow Chows can be stubborn, so it's important to train them early and often. They also have to learn to get along with children and other dogs.

CHOW

Size: Medium. Around 17 to 20 inches tall; weighing between 45 and 70 pounds

Coat: Their thick double coat can be either rough and long or smooth and short.

Coloring: Red, black, blue, cinnamon, and cream

Origin: In ancient China, Chow Chows hunted wolves, sables, and pheasants; pulled carts and sleds; guarded homes; and more.

Famous owners:
TV HOST/PUBLISHER MARTHA STEWART, SINGER JANET JACKSON

BONE-A-FIDE FACTS:

Legend has it that a Chinese emperor from the seventh century kept 2,500 Chow Chows as an army of hunters.

Chow Chows are famous for their jet-black tongues.

Name: COCKER
(AKA "COCKERS")
Group: SPORTING

Temperament: Happy-go-lucky is the best way to describe the Cocker Spaniel. It's sometimes called the "merry Cocker" for that reason. It's a curious pooch that loves adventure and exploring.

Health: With a life span of twelve to fifteen years, Cockers are one of the healthiest breeds. They sometimes suffer from eye problems, as well as issues with their knees and other joints.

Grooming: To keep a cocker's coat shiny and smooth, it needs to be brushed two or three times a week. A haircut will also be required every few months. The eyes and ears must be kept extra clean to prevent infections.

Environment: Cockers can adapt to most climates. As for exercise, a brisk walk or romp in the backyard should keep them happy.

Training: Cockers are extremely intelligent and obedient. If anything, they can be a little too obedient. It's important to use lots of positive reinforcement when training.

BONE-A-FIDE FACTS!

⭐ The word *cocker* comes from woodcock, a type of bird that Cocker Spaniels are very good at retrieving.

⭐ In the 1950s, the Cocker Spaniel was the most popular dog in America, possibly because of the beloved Disney movie *Lady and the Tramp.*

SPANIEL

FAMILY FRIENDLINESS: This breed was made for family life. Its extremely social nature makes it right at home in big, bustling households, especially those with young, energetic kids.

Size: Medium. Between 13 and 15 inches tall; 25 to 30 pounds

Coat: A soft, silky, wavy coat

Coloring: Black, red, brown, and cream

Origin: Ancestors of the Cocker Spaniel date all the way back to the fourteenth century. But the breed we know today developed in England and America in the 1800s, where it was popular with bird hunters.

Famous owners: TALK SHOW HOST OPRAH WINFREY, ACTOR CHARLIZE THERON

Group:

Famous owners:
SINGERS
VANESSA CARLTON
AND FERGIE,
ACTOR
JOSH DUHAMEL,
RETIRED HOCKEY
PLAYER
WAYNE GRETZKY

Environment: Dachshunds can adapt to most climates and homes, although they need moderate exercise.

Training: These little guys and gals are tough and stubborn, but also smart and willing to follow commands.

Temperament: Although descended from fierce hunters, today's Dachshund is known for a playful and lovable nature. They enjoy adventure and will follow their keen sense of smell wherever it leads.

Health: Typical life span is twelve to fourteen years. Their unusually long bodies can lead to spinal problems, especially if they become overweight. A healthy diet and regular exercise are a must.

Grooming: Dachshunds with smooth coats don't require much, but those with wirehaired and longhaired coats need regular brushing and trimming.

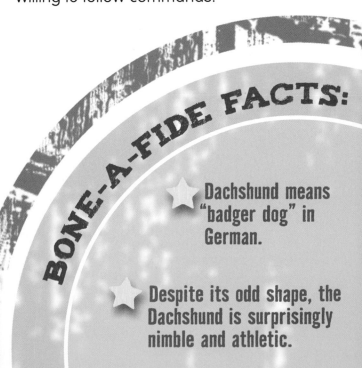

BONE-A-FIDE FACTS:

★ Dachshund means "badger dog" in German.

★ Despite its odd shape, the Dachshund is surprisingly nimble and athletic.

DACHSHUND
(AKA "DOXIE")
HOUND

Size: Small. This hot-dog-shaped breed comes in a standard size (11 to 32 pounds) or miniature (under 11 pounds). Both types feature a long body and short legs.

Coat: Three varieties: smooth, wirehaired, and longhaired

Coloring: A variety of colors, including red, cream, black, chocolate, and gray

Origin: Their long bodies and ferocious spirits were perfect for hunting badgers in Germany during the 1600s.

- Dalmatians are the only breed covered in spots, but they don't have them when they're first born.

- Newborn Dalmatians' fur is all white. It's their skin that has spots, and it's only as they grow up that black or brown fur grows over the skin spots.

BONE-A-FIDE FACTS:

Name:

Group:

Size: Around 2 feet tall; weighs between 40 and 60 pounds

Coat: Short, sleek, and healthy

Coloring: White with black or brown spots. That's what makes a Dalmatian a Dalmatian!

Origin: This breed gets its name from a region in Eastern Europe, although its exact origins are unknown. They were used in Victorian England as coach dogs to lead horse-drawn carriages through the streets. In the United States, they are famous as firehouse dogs.

Famous owner: SINGER PAULA ABDUL

FAMILY FRIENDLINESS: Dals make great pets, especially if there are runners in the family to take them on long jogs. They can be a little too rambunctious for small children.

DALMATIAN
(AKA "DAL")
NONSPORTING

Temperament: Full of energy and intelligence, Dalmatians love to be around people. Since they were bred to run for miles alongside horses, they need to get plenty of exercise to stay happy.

Health: It's not uncommon for a Dalmatian, which has a life span of twelve to fourteen years, to be deaf in at least one ear.

Grooming: Dalmatians shed year-round, but thanks to their short coats, occasional brushing is enough to prevent a house full of dog hair.

Environment: Room to run is the Dalmatian's most important need. It also likes a soft bed and plenty of affection from its master.

Training: This extremely intelligent breed is a quick learner, although it can also be stubborn. Firm but fair training from an early age achieves the best form of obedience.

Name: DOBERMAN
Group: WORKING

FAMILY FRIENDLINESS: Between their loyalty and their watchful, protective natures, Dobermans will do anything to keep their families safe. But if left alone for too long, they can become destructive.

Temperament: Just try sneaking past a Doberman! They are extremely alert, which is why they make such good guard dogs.

Health: Their life span is ten to twelve years. Some suffer from problems with their spines.

Grooming: Their supershort coats require minimal grooming.

Environment: Despite their reputation as guard dogs, Dobermans much prefer to be let indoors at night. They do need plenty of exercise, ideally in a large yard with a tall fence around it.

Training: In the right hands, a Doberman is quick to learn commands and obey every word his or her master speaks.

PINSCHER

Size: Big. From 24 to 28 inches tall; 65 to 90 pounds of pure muscle

Coat: Short, smooth, hard, and thick

Coloring: Usually black with rust-colored markings, they also come in red, fawn, and even blue.

Origin: Legend has it that a German tax collector named Louis Dobermann bred this guard dog to protect him as he made his rounds for work. This breed arrived in America in the early 1900s and quickly became a prized police dog.

Famous owner:
SINGER
MARIAH CAREY

BONE-A-FIDE FACTS:

★ The Doberman is a combination of the Rottweiler, the black-and-tan Terrier, and the short-haired German Pinscher.

★ The Doberman Pinscher is ranked the fifth most intelligent dog in obedience command training.

Name: **FRENCH**
(AKA "FRENCHIE")
Group: **NONSPORTING**

BONE-A-FIDE FACTS:

★ Frenchies are one of the loudest snoring dogs in the world.

★ French bulldogs were bred during the Industrial Revolution to keep English workers company.

BULLDOG

Size: Small. Stands 11 to 13 inches tall; weighs up to 28 pounds

Coat: Short

Coloring: Various colors, including fawn, white, and black

Origin: First bred in England, French Bulldogs are a cross between an English bulldog, a Pug, and a Terrier. They were popularized in Paris, where they got their name.

Temperament: Frenchies were first bred to be companion dogs, and their friendly (but stubborn) temperament is alive and well today.

Health: Their pushed-in faces can lead to breathing issues and eye irritations. Reproducing is a challenge because of their narrow hips and weak legs; they usually require surgery to deliver pups.

Grooming: Very easy, thanks to their short coat. But you do need to keep their face wrinkles dry and free of gunk.

Environment: The perfect city dog, since they don't require a lot of space or exercise. The word "fetch" is definitely not part of the Frenchie's vocabulary!

Famous owners: ACTOR MICHELLE TRACHTENBERG, TV STAR BRODY JENNER

Name: GREAT

Group: WORKING

Size: Big! Around 3 feet tall; can weigh up to 180 pounds!

Coat: Short, thick, and glossy

Coloring: Common colors include tan, fawn, blue, and black

Origin: There's evidence that the Great Dane's ancestry dates back 5,000 years, to ancient Egypt. The Great Dane we know today — a combination of the Irish wolfhound and the English mastiff — has been around for several hundred years.

Temperament: Despite their imposing presence, Great Danes are really gentle giants. Most are caring, sensitive, and playful, which makes them great companions.

Health: They're predisposed to a lot of genetic diseases and have a life span of six to eight years, which is shorter than most breeds.

Grooming: Thanks to that short coat, grooming is minimal with the Great Dane.

Environment: This enormous dog would be out of place in a small apartment. They need a lot of exercise every day.

Training: Like any guard dog, the Great Dane is good at following commands from his or her master. But this dog must be socialized from an early age to become a well-adjusted member of the family.

DANE

FAMILY FRIENDLINESS: Great Danes love all people, even children. But because of their size and strength, they should never be left unattended around babies and small children.

Famous owners:
ACTOR AMERICA FERRERA, BASEBALL PLAYER MARK MCGWIRE

BONE-A-FIDE FACTS:

★ The Great Dane is so massive, it's known as the "King of Dogs."

★ The Great Dane was originally bred to hunt wild boar, a very ferocious animal. But now Great Danes are just great companions.

Name: **IRISH**
Group: **SPORTING**

Famous owner:
PRESIDENT
RICHARD NIXON

FAMILY FRIENDLINESS: This extremely outgoing breed thrives in big, active families. But it can be a little rowdy for small children.

BONE-A-FIDE FACTS!

When they were first bred, Irish Setters' fur was a combination of red and white, but today they're all red, all the time.

It's believed that Irish Setters have a dash of five different breeds, but no one knows for certain.

SETTER

Size: Big. Two feet tall; between 60 and 70 pounds

Coat: Its straight, shiny coat is the Irish Setter's defining feature.

Coloring: Mahogany red

Origin: The exact origin of the Irish Setter is unknown, but they became popular in Ireland in the eighteenth century, where they were used to hunt birds.

Temperament: Irish Setters are known for their outgoing, goofy personalities. They were bred for tireless hunting, which means their energy is pretty much boundless. That's why they do best with owners who enjoy lots of activity.

Health: Irish Setters will live for twelve to fourteen years. They are prone to bloating.

Grooming: That luxurious coat needs to be brushed and combed every few days. Careful attention to the feet, ears, and eyes is also recommended.

Environment: This breed can adapt to most climates. It needs plenty of room to run, so it's not suited to apartment life. At least an hour of exercise every day is recommended.

Training: A stable, eager-to-please temperament makes this breed easy to train.

Name: LABRADOR
(AKA "LAB")
Group: SPORTING

Size: Medium. About 2 feet tall; up to 80 pounds

Coat: A layered, oily coat keeps them warm in cold weather.

Coloring: Labs come in three colors: black (the most common), yellow, and chocolate. Silver is a fourth color, but it's extremely rare.

Origin: First bred in Newfoundland by fishermen in the early 1800s to retrieve fishing nets and even fish that had gotten away, these dogs were named after the Labrador Sea in which they worked.

BONE-A-FIDE FACTS:

★ Thanks to their webbed feet and otterlike tails, Labs can swim twice as fast as ducks.

★ The Labrador Retriever's strong legs help them jump far — twenty-seven feet is the current record!

FAMILY FRIENDLINESS: Labs are fantastic family pets, making them the most popular breed of dog in the United States right now.

RETRIEVER

Temperament: This big, friendly dog is full of life. Its desire to please makes it an excellent guide dog or rescue dog, not to mention a loving and loyal companion.

Health: This vibrant breed will live for twelve to thirteen years, but like all large dogs, it is prone to joint issues, especially around the hips and knees.

Grooming: While Labs do shed in the fall and spring, they don't require a lot more than occasional brushing.

Environment: Well suited to any climate, especially the cold, Labs are high-energy dogs that need room to roam. They shouldn't be cooped up in a small apartment.

Training: The Lab is among the smartest of all breeds, able to learn up to 300 commands. That makes for easy training, but it's important to start when they're pups.

Famous owners:
PRESIDENT BILL CLINTON, ACTORS BEN AFFLECK AND JENNIFER GARNER

Name: MALTESE
Group: TOY

Temperament: The Maltese is one of the most pampered breeds on the planet — and that's just the way they like it! This natural-born companion dog loves nothing more than to sit on the lap of its owner, or get carted from place to place in a carrying bag.

Health: Despite their delicate looks, Maltese are surprisingly robust. They have a lot of dental issues, however, so it's recommended that you brush their teeth three to seven times a week.

Grooming: Looking good doesn't come easy. If you own a Maltese, you'll need to brush it every day and bathe it weekly to keep its coat gorgeous.

Environment: Maltese may love to be pampered, but they can also adapt well to most climates. The one thing they don't do well with is long climbs. If you love to hike, this isn't the breed for you.

Training: Because Maltese form such close connections with their owners, it's important to teach them to be independent from a young age. Otherwise they'll bark and yelp nonstop anytime their owner leaves the room.

BONE-A-FIDE FACTS:

★ The Maltese is the world's oldest lapdog.

★ The famous hotel tycoon Leona Helmsey left twelve million dollars to her Maltese, Trouble.

Famous owners: FRENCH QUEEN MARIE ANTOINETTE, ACTORS EVA LONGORIA PARKER AND LINDSAY LOHAN

Size: Small. Between 4 and 7 pounds; about 10 inches tall

Coat: A hair coat, which means they don't shed as much as other breeds — a plus for people with allergies

Coloring: Pure white

Origin: One of the oldest breeds, the Maltese was first bred on the island of Malta. It's hard to believe because of their tiny size, but Maltese descended from working dogs.

FAMILY FRIENDLINESS: Like a lot of small dogs, Maltese don't always like to be around young children.

Name: MINI
(AKA "MIN PIN")

Group: TOY

Size: Small. Roughly 10 inches tall; 8 to 10 pounds

Coat: Smooth, hard, and short

Coloring: Red, chocolate and rust, black and rust

Origin: The Min Pin was first bred in Germany in the seventeenth century to chase rats and other rodents away from barnyards. Today, it is one of the most popular toy breeds in the United States.

PINSCHER

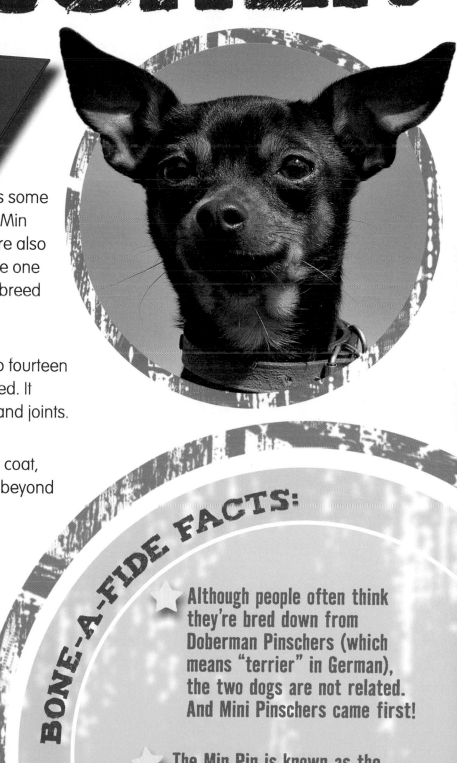

Temperament: Often referred to as some of the world's most energetic dogs, Min Pins are bursting with energy. They're also fearless, so don't be surprised to see one of these little guys take on a bigger breed at the dog run.

Health: With a life span of twelve to fourteen years, this is a relatively healthy breed. It sometimes has issues with its hips and joints.

Grooming: Thanks to its supershort coat, Min Pins need almost no grooming beyond the occasional brushing and bath.

Environment: Min Pins are always on the go, but since they're so small, an apartment provides ample room to run. This breed does not do well in the cold, so sunny climates only, please!

Training: Smart but stubborn, they can be trained, but it takes some doing.

BONE-A-FIDE FACTS:

Although people often think they're bred down from Doberman Pinschers (which means "terrier" in German), the two dogs are not related. And Mini Pinschers came first!

The Min Pin is known as the "King of the Toys."

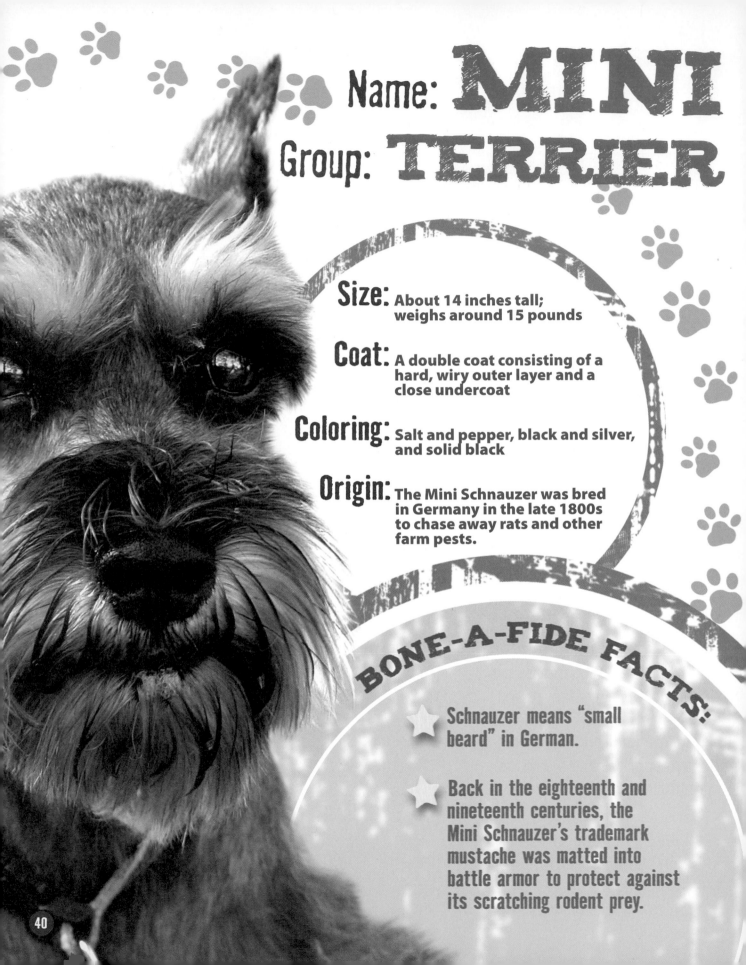

Name: **MINI**
Group: **TERRIER**

Size: About 14 inches tall; weighs around 15 pounds

Coat: A double coat consisting of a hard, wiry outer layer and a close undercoat

Coloring: Salt and pepper, black and silver, and solid black

Origin: The Mini Schnauzer was bred in Germany in the late 1800s to chase away rats and other farm pests.

BONE-A-FIDE FACTS:

⭐ Schnauzer means "small beard" in German.

⭐ Back in the eighteenth and nineteenth centuries, the Mini Schnauzer's trademark mustache was matted into battle armor to protect against its scratching rodent prey.

SCHNAUZER

Temperament: Alert, active, and playful, Mini Schnauzers are one of the most popular terrier pets. They're also fearless, but not aggressive toward other dogs.

Health: This generally healthy breed will normally live between twelve and fourteen years. They do sometimes have problems with kidney stones.

Grooming: Its distinctive coat needs to be brushed once or twice a week and trimmed every couple of weeks.

Environment: Mini Schnauzers can adapt to most environments, and they're equally happy in a city apartment or a home in the suburbs, provided they get lots of exercise and plenty of affection.

Training: Extremely obedient and quick to learn, a Mini Schnauzer wants nothing more than to please its owner.

FAMILY FRIENDLINESS: Mini Schnauzers love to be part of the family, especially families that have lots of rowdy kids to romp around with. They make excellent guard dogs.

41

Name: NEWFOUNDLAND
(AKA "NEWFIES")
Group: WORKING

Temperament: Despite their massive size, Newfies are famous for their calm, sweet, and amiable dispositions. They are extremely loyal and protective, so they may become aggressive if they think their owners are in danger. Otherwise, they're true gentle giants.

Health: Newfies can live for about ten years. Some suffer from bloating and joint problems.

Grooming: To keep the thick coat looking plush, Newfies should be brushed twice a week, especially during the shedding season. They're big droolers and sloppy drinkers, so be prepared to do some cleaning up after them.

Environment: Newfies thrive in cold climates. They do not do well in extreme heat. This big, active dog needs lots of room to romp around.

Training: Newfies are intelligent, patient, and eager to please. Provided training starts when they're pups, they will be extremely obedient and learn many commands.

Size: Over 2 feet in height; weighing upward of 150 pounds. That's one big dog!

Coat: A thick double coat — a soft undercoat and a coarse, straight outercoat

Coloring: Solid black, brown, or gray, or a mix of black and white

Origin: Bred by fishermen on the coast of Newfoundland in Canada, Newfies were used to haul heavy fishing nets through icy waters and timber from the thick forests.

FAMILY FRIENDLINESS:
This giant beast fits right into any family, even ones with young children. The only requirement is lots of love and exercise.

BONE-A-FIDE FACTS:

Newfies have webbed feet designed for long-distance swimming.

Newfies are legendary for pulling drowning victims safely to shore. One saved the French emperor Napoleon Bonaparte when he fell overboard a ship off the coast of Italy.

Famous owners:
THIS BREED WAS BELOVED BY MANY U.S. PRESIDENTS, INCLUDING JAMES BUCHANAN, ULYSSES S. GRANT, AND RUTHERFORD B. HAYES.

Name: OLD

Famous owners:
PRESIDENT FRANKLIN DELANO ROOSEVELT, SINGER PAUL McCARTNEY

Temperament: This jolly giant is extremely friendly toward family and strangers alike. Its clownish personality is a big part of its appeal.

Health: They can live up to ten years. But be warned, they are fond of chasing cars, so it's extra important to keep them on a leash when walking them on the street.

Grooming: The sheepdog's shaggy coat must be brushed every other day. Lots of stuff gets caught in that thick coat, including sticks, leaves, and other debris.

Environment: These big dogs love to roam around. A big yard or a nearby park is a major plus for Old English Sheepdog owners.

Training: With heads that big, it's no wonder sheepdogs can be a little headstrong. But in general they are quite willing to be trained.

ENGLISH SHEEPDOG

Group: HERDING

Size: Big. Approximately 22 inches tall; weighs 60 to 90 pounds

Coat: Long and shaggy coat

Coloring: Any combination of gray, blue, and white

Origin: Bred in nineteenth-century England, Old English Sheepdogs herded sheep and cattle and also defended livestock from the ferocious wolves that roamed the countryside.

BONE-A-FIDE FACTS:

In the movie *The Little Mermaid*, Prince Eric's loyal companion is an Old English Sheepdog.

The famous Beatles song "Martha My Dear" was inspired by Paul McCartney's Old English Sheepdog.

45

Name: PEKINGESE
Group: TOY

Temperament: These pint-sized pooches are anything but passive. In fact, they possess a lion-like courage and self-esteem. They can be playful and loving, but don't expect them to play fetch or cuddle on the couch for hours.

Health: The Pekingese is one of the healthiest breeds. They can live for thirteen to fifteen years if cared for properly, though their broad, flat faces can sometimes lead to breathing problems.

Grooming: Brush and comb your Pekingese's mane-like coat for at least one hour every week. Their wrinkled faces must also be wiped clean regularly to prevent infections.

Environment: Pekingese are perfect apartment dogs. They need daily exercise, but a romp between rooms will generally do the trick. Pekingese can suffer from heat exhaustion, so they do better in colder climates.

Training: Obedience school is highly recommended from an early age for these famously stubborn and strong-willed dogs. They can also be a little hard to house-train.

BONE-A-FIDE FACTS!

⭐ The Pekingese used to be called "sleeve dogs" because they could fit up the sleeves of their masters.

⭐ For centuries, this breed was only for wealthy Chinese, but now they're adored by all.

Size: Small. About 9 inches tall; weighs around 14 pounds

Coat: A double coat that consists of a long, straight outer layer and a thick, soft undercoat

Coloring: Ranges from blond to beige to brown muzzles

Origin: Chinese Buddhists idolized the lion, so back in ancient times they bred a miniature version of the regal beast. The result was the imperial Pekingese.

FAMILY FRIENDLINESS: Devotion isn't out of the question, but they don't show affection as readily as other breeds.

Famous owners: COMEDIAN JOAN RIVERS, QUEEN VICTORIA OF ENGLAND

Name: POODLE

Group: TOY

FAMILY FRIENDLINESS: Because of their intelligence and pleasant dispositions, Poodles are great for families who have a lot of time to spend with their pet.

Size: Poodles come in three sizes: full (15 inches or over), mini (10 to 15 inches), and toy (6 to 10 inches).

Coat: Poodles have what's known as a hair coat. They don't shed, so they're good dogs for people with allergies.

Coloring: A variety of colors, including black, blue, gray, silver, cream, and white

Origin: Poodles were bred to be hunting dogs in northern Europe.

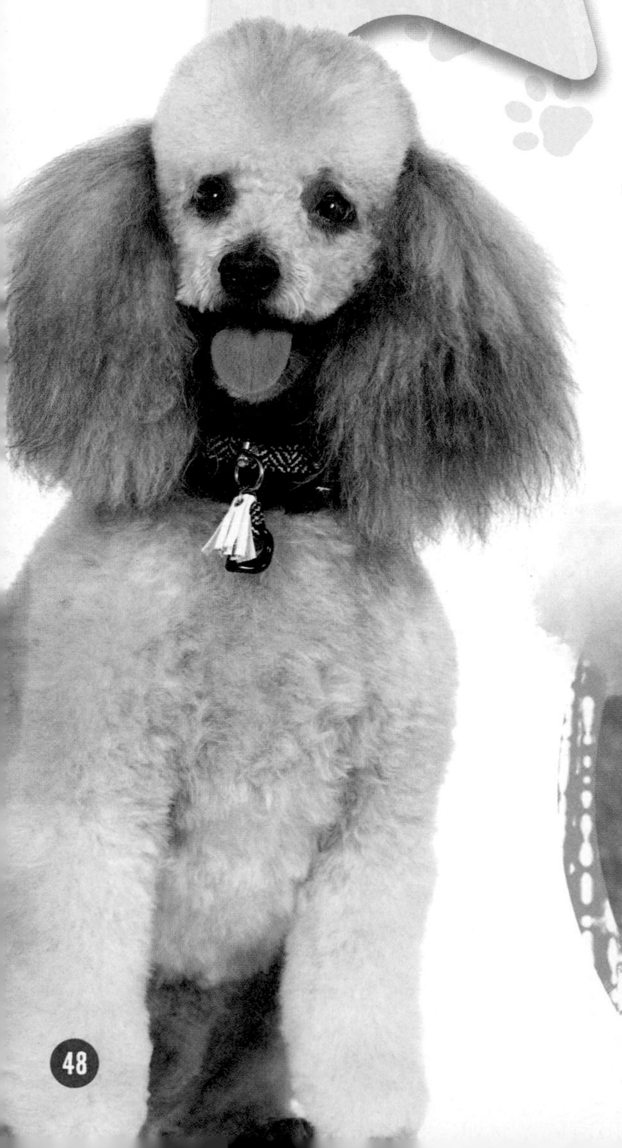

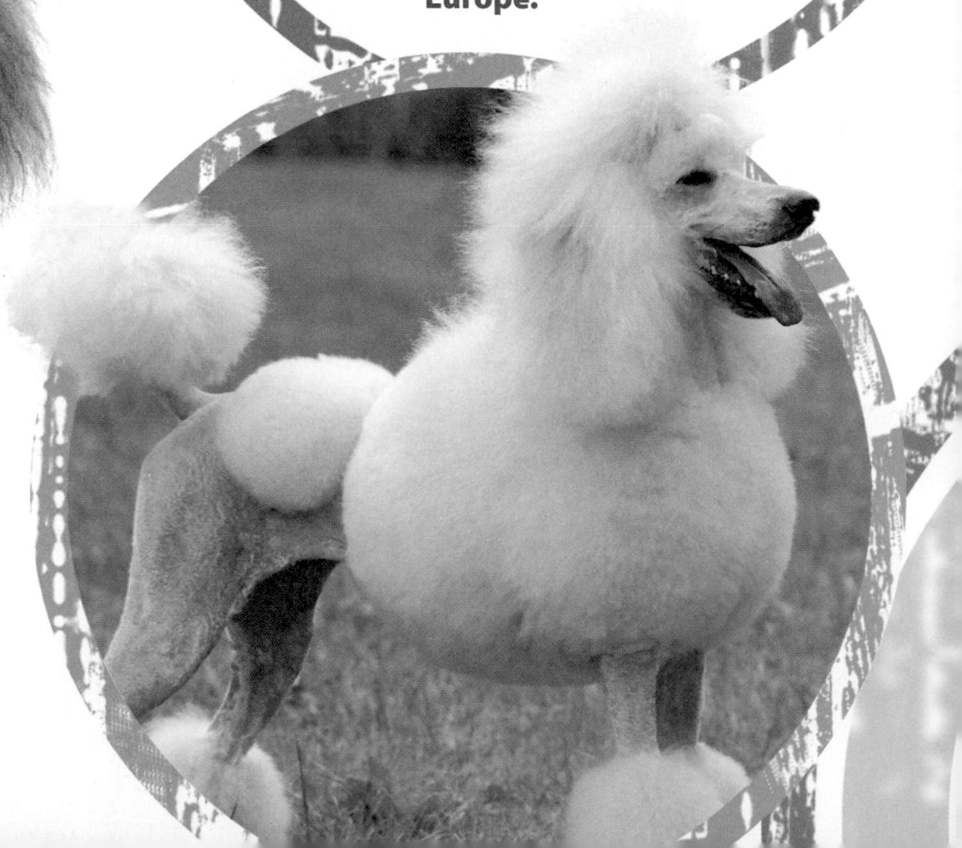

Temperament: Poodles are super smart, perhaps second only to the Border Collie in intelligence.

Health: If they get plenty of exercise and maintain a healthy diet, Poodles can live for ten years or longer.

Grooming: Extremely high maintenance. They should get a bath every few weeks. Their clip styles — that is, the way their coats are cut — demand constant attention.

Environment: Poodles are very active breeds. They need a lot of space and exercise.

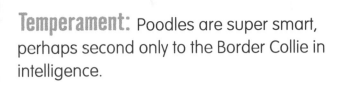

Famous owners:
ACTORS
VANESSA HUDGENS
AND ELLEN POMPEO

BONE-A-FIDE FACTS:

⭐ A Poodle crossed with a Labrador Retriever is called a Labradoodle.

⭐ A Poodle crossed with a Cocker Spaniel is called a Cockapoo.

Name: PUG

Group: TOY

Size: Small. About 10 inches tall; 15 to 20 pounds

Coat: Soft, short-haired

Coloring: Black, fawn, silver fawn, and apricot fawn

Origin: First bred in ancient China, the Pug was a favorite in Buddhist monasteries.

FAMILY FRIENDLINESS: Pugs are one of the best dogs for kids. Moms and dads like them too.

Famous owners:
ACTORS TORI SPELLING AND JESSICA ALBA

Temperament: Energetic, happy, and adaptable. Pugs were originally bred to be companions for the emperor in ancient China, and their loyal, lovable personalities have survived through the ages. If a dog is man's best friend, the Pug is more like a BFF!

Health: The average life span of Pugs is twelve to fifteen years. But

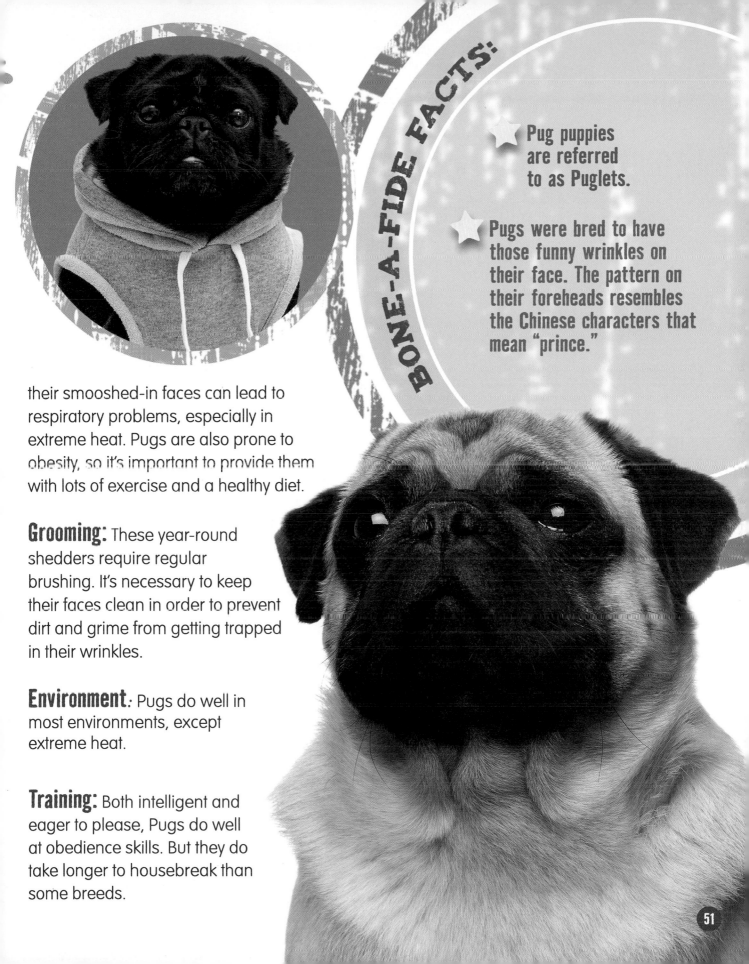

Pug puppies are referred to as Puglets.

Pugs were bred to have those funny wrinkles on their face. The pattern on their foreheads resembles the Chinese characters that mean "prince."

their smooshed-in faces can lead to respiratory problems, especially in extreme heat. Pugs are also prone to obesity, so it's important to provide them with lots of exercise and a healthy diet.

Grooming: These year-round shedders require regular brushing. It's necessary to keep their faces clean in order to prevent dirt and grime from getting trapped in their wrinkles.

Environment: Pugs do well in most environments, except extreme heat.

Training: Both intelligent and eager to please, Pugs do well at obedience skills. But they do take longer to housebreak than some breeds.

Name: RHODESIAN
Group: HOUND

Size: Around 25 inches tall; weighs between 70 and 85 pounds

Coat: Short, sleek, and glossy

Coloring: Light wheaten to red wheaten ("wheaten" is a color that resembles wheat)

Origin: This native of South Africa was bred as a hunting and guard dog. In the 1870s, it was taken to the neighboring country, Rhodesia, where big-game hunters revered its keen vision and sense of smell. Ridgebacks are best known for the ridge of hair on their backs, which gives them their name.

BONE-A-FIDE FACTS!

⭐ Ridgebacks were once called "lion hounds" because they were fast and brave enough to hunt lions in Africa.

⭐ Ridgebacks can keep up with a running horse for up to thirty miles!

RIDGEBACK

Temperament: This "people dog" craves human interaction. They especially enjoy getting cozy on the couch with their owners. They're also powerful and protective, which makes them excellent guard dogs, but also means they can be aggressive toward strangers and other dogs.

Health: With a life span of ten to thirteen years, Ridgebacks are generally healthy. Overeating can be an issue, so it's important to keep them on a healthy diet.

Grooming: Thanks to their short, smooth coats, Ridgebacks require very little grooming.

Environment: Ridgebacks adapt well to most climates, but they like to sleep indoors (in bed with their masters if possible!). They need plenty of exercise, preferably in the form of long runs or hikes. They are not the best city dogs.

Training: This intelligent breed responds well to training. But it can also be strong-willed, so obedience school is strongly recommended.

Famous owners:
VOLLEYBALL STAR GABRIEL REECE, ACTOR PATRICK SWAYZE

Name: # SAINT

Group: # WORKING

Size: Big. Can weigh up to 200 pounds and stand 28 inches tall. They have an incredibly powerful build.

Coat: Either short, dense, and coarse or long, soft, and wavy

Coloring: A variety of colors, ranging from white to deep brown to red to yellow

Origin: Although it has ancient roots, the Saint Bernard we know today became popular in seventeenth-century Switzerland, where it worked pulling carts and performing other heavy labor. Monks in the Swiss Alps soon discovered the dogs' ability to find their way through heavy snow, and they were put to work rescuing travelers lost in severe weather.

Famous owner: CARTOON CHARACTER DONALD DUCK

FAMILY FRIENDLINESS: In the right family, Saint Bernards make an excellent pet. They can be stubborn, so you'll need to train them well and exercise patience. Saint Bernards are gentle with children, but they're not always very playful.

BERNARD

Temperament: You might expect a dog this big to be a bully. But in fact, Saint Bernards are very calm, gentle, and easygoing.

Health: Their life span of eight to ten years is shorter than most. Bloating and heart disease are concerns. Young puppies are prone to obesity, so watch their diets closely.

Grooming: Whether short-haired or long, Saint Bernards need to be brushed weekly, and more frequently during the shedding season. They drool a lot.

Environment: This big dog needs a big environment, such as the country or a home in the suburbs with a spacious, fenced-in yard. Bred for cold, snowy climates, they can't tolerate the heat.

Training: Because of their size, all Saint Bernards should go to obedience school so they learn not to knock over small children or steal food off tabletops.

BONE-A-FIDE FACTS:

★ The breed is named after Saint Bernard Hospice, a refuge for travelers crossing between Switzerland and France.

★ Saint Bernards have saved more than 2,000 lives. When they find lost travelers in the snow, they lick their face and lie beside them to keep them warm.

★ The most famous Saint Bernard of all is a dog named Barry, who rescued forty people.

Name: SHIH

Group: TOY

Size: Small. 8 to 11 inches tall; 9 to 16 pounds

Coat: A distinctive long, flowing double coat. The hair on the top of its head is often tied in a bow.

Coloring: Usually a combination of many colors, including white, brown, and black

Origin: Like the Pekingese, the Shih Tzu was bred by Chinese Buddhists to resemble a smaller version of this culture's much-revered lion.

TZU

Temperament: Bred for companionship, Shih Tzus are exceptionally outgoing, sweet, and good-natured. Like many small dogs, they can be rather strong-willed.

Health: This breed is known for its general good health, and will live between eleven and fourteen years.

Grooming: That luxurious coat needs plenty of care. It should be combed and brushed every other day, and trimmed occasionally.

Environment: This active breed needs daily exercise, but indoor romping is often enough. That makes the Shih Tzu a favorite apartment pet. It does not do well in hot weather, so temperate to cold climates are preferred.

Training: Although these palace pooches can be stubborn and demanding, they respond well to training — as long as you start early.

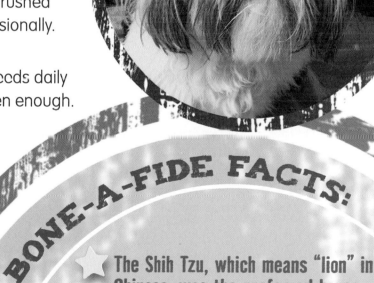

BONE-A-FIDE FACTS:

⭐ The Shih Tzu, which means "lion" in Chinese, was the preferred house pet throughout most of the Ming Dynasty, which ruled China between the fourteenth and seventeenth centuries.

⭐ For such a small dog, the Shih Tzu is surprisingly strong and sturdy.

Name: SOFT-COATED WHEATEN TERRIER

Group: TERRIER

Temperament: Extremely outgoing, energetic, and spunky. Their tendency to flop around makes them seem like little clowns.

Health: Wheaten Terriers are hardy breeds, although they are very allergic to fleas. A single bite can lead to a full-blown skin rash. The breed also has trouble digesting protein, so they are vulnerable to weight loss.

Grooming: The downside of this breed's glorious coat is that it requires a lot of attention. You'll need to brush the coat daily and provide frequent baths.

Environment: Wheaten Terriers do well in any climate. It's a great dog for people with small homes. But it also requires a lot of exercise to release all that pent-up energy.

Training: Provided you start early enough, Wheaten Terriers are easy to train.

Famous owners:
SINGER JOSH GROBAN,
ACTORS ALI LARTER
AND AMY SMART

TERRIER

Size: Medium. Around 19 inches tall; up to 40 pounds

Coat: A luxurious, silken coat with a blond tuft of hair over the eyes and a long beard beneath the chin

Coloring: Gold, wheaten fur, though pups are rusty brown

Origin: Wheaten Terriers were first bred as working dogs on farms in Ireland. They are the fourth terrier of Irish descent, joining the Kerry Blue, the Irish, and the Glen of Imaal. Wheatens didn't reach the shores of the United States until the 1960s.

FAMILY FRIENDLINESS: Soft-Coated Wheaten Terriers are extremely good-natured. They love to be part of a family, preferably a big one with lots of energetic kids to roll around with.

BONE-A-FIDE FACTS:

⭐ Wheaten pups aren't born wheaten at all, but a rusty brown color. It's only when they outgrow the puppy stage that their hair turns wheaten blond.

⭐ When a Wheaten gets injured, the fur grows back brown in the spot, like a bruise, before returning to its usual golden color.

Name: WEST HIGHLAND WHITE TERRIER
(AKA "WESTIE")

Group: TERRIER

Famous owner:
ACTOR
ROBERT PATTINSON

Grooming: The stiff coat must be brushed two or three times a week. It's also important to pluck the dead undercoat, a process known as stripping.

Environment: It's in the Westie's nature to chase birds, rabbits, and even cats, so they need to be kept on a leash or in a yard with a fence. They're small enough to live in an apartment.

Temperament: Westies may be small in stature but they have huge personalities. This is one of the friendliest of the Terrier breeds, but also one of the strongest willed.

Health: Terriers tend to be hardy breeds, and the Westie is no exception. It can live twelve to fourteen years, although some are prone to problems with the hips and joints.

Training: Westies can be stubborn, and they LOVE to dig. But provided training starts as pups, they'll grow into obedient dogs who don't tear up the backyard. Just don't expect them to stop chasing small animals!

Size: Small. Around 10 inches tall; weighs 15 to 20 pounds

Coat: A double coat: a straight, stiff outer layer and a shorter underlayer

Coloring: Snow white

Origin: First bred in the Scottish highlands, Westies helped hunt foxes, badgers, and other small animals.

BONE-A-FIDE FACTS:

⭐ According to legend, the Westie was given its pure white color so that it wouldn't be mistakenly shot by hunters in the field.

⭐ Westies were first called Poltalloch Terriers, after the town in Scotland where they were originally bred.

Name: YORKSHIRE
Group: TOY

Size: Small. About 8 or 9 inches; weighs just 7 pounds or less

Coat: Long and silky, often with the top tuft tied in a bow

Coloring: Usually a combination of tan and steel blue

Origin: Although they look dainty, Yorkies were actually bred in nineteenth-century England to catch rats!

BONE-A-FIDE FACTS:

⭐ In the beginning, Yorkies were looked down upon by the wealthy because of their working-class roots. These days, they're adored by the rich and famous.

⭐ Yorkies are brave! They've been known to take on dogs ten times their size.

TERRIER (AKA "YORKIE")

FAMILY FRIENDLINESS: With sufficient pampering, Yorkies are exceedingly affectionate and devoted family members. Because of their tiny size, they're excellent travel companions.

Temperament: Yorkies definitely have small-dog syndrome: They think they're much bigger than their actual size.

Health: With a typical life span of fifteen to sixteen years, Yorkies live longer than most dogs. They occasionally suffer from problems with their hips and joints.

Grooming: If these dogs were humans, they'd be regulars at the hair salon. Their luxurious coats must be combed and brushed at least every other day, if not daily.

Environment: Ideal for apartment living, Yorkies are popular city dogs. They can adapt to most climates — maybe because they tend to spend much of their time indoors.

Training: True to their Terrier roots, Yorkies often have a stubborn streak. They are big yappers but can be trained to stop.

POP QUIZ!

Test your pup proficiency! Answer the questions below. Then check the answers on the bottom of the page to see if you're at the head of the canine class.

1. This breed has the strongest sense of smell of all dogs.
A. Irish Setter
B. Bloodhound
C. Pekingese
D. Yorkshire Terrier

2. Webbed feet and an otterlike tail make this one of the fastest canine swimmers.
A. Akita
B. Maltese
C. Labrador Retriever
D. Dachshund

3. Mexican royalty once used this dog like a hot-water bottle.
A. Chihuahua
B. Shih Tzu
C. Newfoundland
D. Yorkshire Terrier

4. This dog has the longest ears of any breed.
A. Beagle
B. Dalmatian
C. Basset Hound
D. Mini Schnauzer

5. The most popular breed in America today
A. Labrador Retriever
B. Beagle
C. Chihuahua
D. Bulldog

6. How many recognized breeds of dog are there in the world today?
A. 55
B. 102
C. 163
D. 290

7. This breed is famous for rescuing travelers caught in blizzards.
A. Rhodesian Ridgeback
B. Airedale Terrier
C. Great Dane
D. Saint Bernard

8. Despite its name, this breed is actually brown when it's a puppy.
A. Dalmatian
B. Golden Retriever
C. Irish Setter
D. Soft-Coated Wheaten Terrier

9. Robert Pattinson has this dog for a pet.
A. Saint Bernard
B. Chihuahua
C. Chow Chow
D. West Highland White Terrier

10. The name of this breed means "lion" in Chinese.
A. Maltese
B. Shih Tzu
C. Doberman Pinscher
D. Pekingese

11. This breed's name means "badger dog" in German.
A. Shih Tzu
B. Newfoundland
C. Dachshund
D. Chow Chow

12. A line of raised hair running along its spine defines this breed.
A. Rhodesian Ridgeback
B. Pug
C. Soft-Coated Wheaten Terrier
D. Old English Sheepdog

13. What breed is most commonly associated with firemen?
A. Yorkshire Terrier
B. Great Dane
C. Akita
D. Dalmatian

14. Its thick, shaggy coat sets this breed apart.
A. Rhodesian Ridgeback
B. Old English Sheepdog
C. Bloodhound
D. Soft-Coated Wheaten Terrier

15. This breed may be second only to the Border Collie in intelligence.
A. Airedale Terrier
B. Irish Setter
C. Poodle
D. Pekingese

What your scores mean:
11 to 15 correct:
You're a doggone expert! If you don't already own a pooch, you should!

6 to 10 correct:
You're hot on the scent to being a bone-a-fide dog lover.

1 to 5 correct:
Dog and man may be best friends, but right now you're more like close acquaintances.

0 correct:
Oh well. There's always a cat!

Answers: 1. b, **2.** c, **3.** a, **4.** c, **5.** a, **6.** c, **7.** d, **8.** d, **9.** d, **10.** b, **11.** c, **12.** a, **13.** d, **14.** b, **15.** c